Ebony Sea

by Irene Smalls

Illustrated by Jon Onye Lockard

LONGMEADOW PRESS

I love you, Black child

—I.S.

*To my family and the countless Africans
lost in the Atlantic Ocean during the
Middle Passage*

—J.O.L.

Library of Congress Cataloging-in-Publication Data
Smalls-Hector, Irene. Ebony sea / by Irene Smalls ; illustrated by Jon Onye Lockard. — 1st ed.
p. cm.
Summary: A story based on accounts of an incident in South Carolina of Igbo resistance to slavery.
ISBN 0-681-00679-X
[1. Igbo (African people)—Fiction. 2. Slave-trade—South Carolina—Fiction. 3. Wateree River (S.C.)—Fiction.]
I. Lockard, Jon, ill. II. Title.
PZ7.S63915E1 1995   95-25858
[FIC] DC20   CIP
                                  AC

Book design by Allison G. Russo

ISBN: 0-681-00679-X

Manufactured in Singapore
First Edition
0 9 8 7 6 5 4 3 2 1

Sources:

Raymond A. and Alice Bauer, *"Day to Day Resistance to Slavery," Journal of Negro History* 27, Association for the study of Negro Life & History, Inc.(Oct. 1942) 388-419.

Blacks in White America: Before 1865, edited by Robert V. Haynes, (New York: David McKay Co.,1972), 254.

My folks don't want me to talk about Slavery, edited by Belinda Hurmence. (Winston-Salem, N.C.: John F. Blair, 1984), 61.

"My folks don't wants me to talk bout slavery. They's shame we ever was slaves," said Sarah Debro, once a slave in North Carolina. I wrote *Ebony Sea* because so many people are ashamed of American Black slavery. I wrote *Ebony Sea* because the action of the Africans of Ebo Landing exemplified the great courage and fierce pride of some of those Africans consigned to be slaves. They ended their lives with a bold and terrible act. But I believe it was an act born of love: love of home, love of country, and love of family.

Most importantly *Ebony Sea* is about those Africans like Benriver who lived. Who lived to tell the stories, dream the dreams, and sing the songs. They were brave people too. The day to day courage it took to work under such horrific conditions, to love and to be loved, to survive and to multiply, is an obstinate strength that has never been fully recognized or appreciated. I offer this story as a tribute to my ancestors. From those first Africans came jazz, Dunbar, Du Bois, Morrison and Miles.

J. S.

Boston, February 22, 1995

THIS STORY WAS INSPIRED BY ACCOUNTS OF AN INCIDENT THAT OCCURRED IN THE DAYS OF AFRICAN-AMERICAN SLAVERY, WHEN A SHIP CARRYING AFRICAN SLAVES TO AMERICA DOCKED ON ONE OF THE SEA ISLANDS OFF THE COAST OF GEORGIA. IT IS SAID THAT THIS GROUP OF SLAVES, KNOWN AS EBOS, RESISTED THE LIFE THAT AWAITED THEM BY WALKING INTO THE RIVER AND DROWNING THEMSELVES.

There is a place that is like no other place.

There was a day that was like no other day.

There is a man who is like no other man. Benriver is his name.
Say his name flat and it is Benriver. Say it round and it is Been
to the River because that is where you find him most days, sitting
at Ebo Landing on the banks of the Wateree River. Benriver is
part spirit. He can fly. But he doesn't fly anymore, not after that
day, the day the sea turned ebony.

The slaves heard tell of another big ship coming, coming across the great water. They heard tell of another big ship coming and they cried when they heard of it.

And the waves kept rolling, to and fro, to and fro.
Swoosh, swash, swish, swoosh, swash, swish,
splish, splash, splish-splash,
splatter.

Finally the day of the ship's arrival came. Its cargo was a large group of Ebos from the African coast, sent across the sea to become slaves. Men, women, children, and babies, young, old, highborn and low. Out of the hold in the bowels of that crude filthy ship they came in chains, shackled, yoked, tied, fettered, wrapped, and choking.

And the waves kept rolling,
to and fro,
to and fro.
Swoosh, swash, swish,
swoosh, swash, swish,
splish, splash,
splish-splash,
splatter.

enriver was the last of the Ebo slaves
for those plantations. He had been the ship's
cabin boy then, a mere chip of mahogany wood.

*T*his group of Africans was different from the others. There were no cries heard, no screams. They were silent. So silent that the group of seasoned slaves sent out to get them off the ship at first didn't know what to make of it and hung back.

The Africans from the ship moved slowly at first, slowly, sluggishly. Until, out from the bottom of the crowd, the leader came. A little bit of a thing, a woman. At the head of this crowd of kings and clowns, babes and brawny men, was a small woman with her head held so high and so proud it looked as if it were made of the blackest onyx stone. Suddenly the group began to move faster,

step, step,

step, step,

step, step.

And the waves
kept rolling,
to and fro,
to and fro.
Swoosh, swash, swish,
swoosh, swash, swish,
splish, splash,
splish-splash,
splatter.

*T*his dark, dark onyx-faced woman wore her *tignon,* or head kerchief, proudly. She carried herself like a queen with her red kerchief on her head. Everyone could see that she was a royal slave. One of the other slaves whispered, "She shore can tote herself. They musta stole her from Africa with that red handkerchief." She came walking and a hush fell over the crowd. Her skirts swished and swayed as she moved. Everyone stepped back to let her pass. The air stood still. The sun did not dare move.

And the waves kept rolling, to and fro, to and fro.

    Swoosh, swash, swish,

        swoosh, swash, swish,

            splish, splash,

          splish-splash,

        splatter.

She walked out
and they all
came behind.

That proud woman, that
African queen, stepped
down those wooden
planks onto the shore.
Step, step, step, step.

She wanted to go home.
Her yearning toward Africa
had grown so great.

Step, step,
step, step.

She stopped.
She looked around
and saw it all—
the past, the present
and the future.

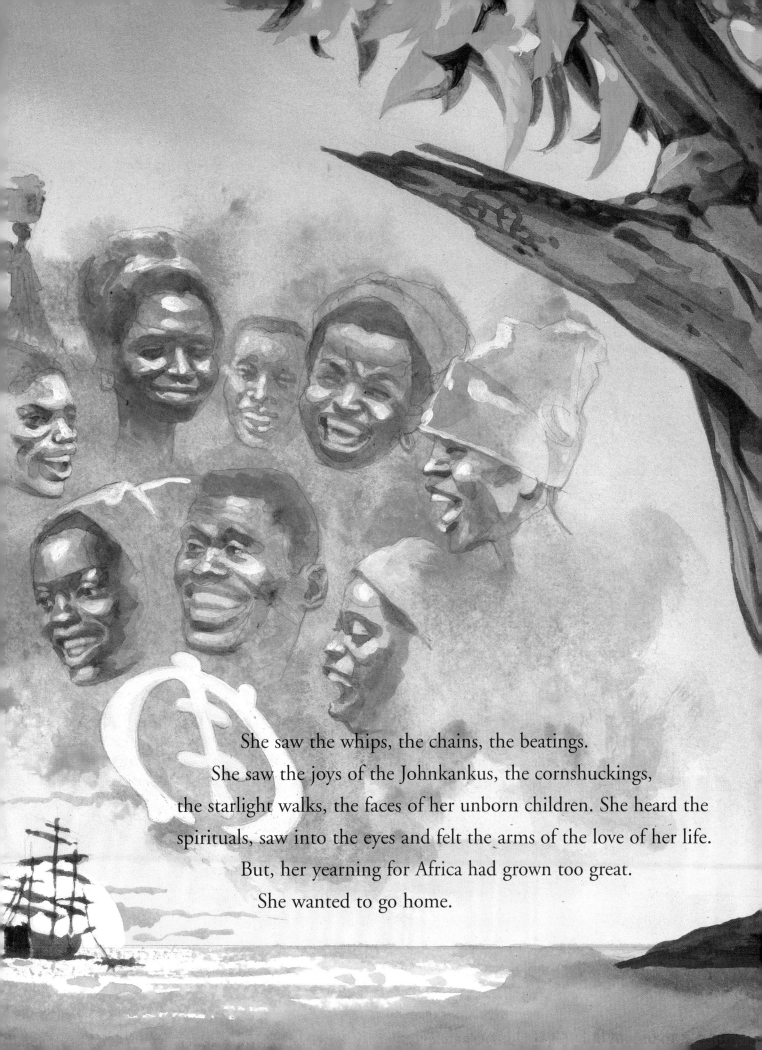

She saw the whips, the chains, the beatings.
She saw the joys of the Johnkankus, the cornshuckings,
the starlight walks, the faces of her unborn children. She heard the
spirituals, saw into the eyes and felt the arms of the love of her life.
But, her yearning for Africa had grown too great.
She wanted to go home.

And the waves kept rolling, to and fro, to and fro.

Swoosh, swash, swish,

swoosh, swash, swish,

splish, splash, splish-splash,

splatter.

And then she did it. She turned and walked through the tall tall grass, into the boundary between land and sea, onto the water covered sand, and then into the depths, the deepest depths, of the Wateree River, deeper and deeper without uttering a sound. In her Ebo beliefs an African who dies goes back home to Africa. She wanted to go home.

And they all followed her without a word.

They had cried when they were taken from their fathers. They had cried when they were ripped from their mothers. They had cried when they were snatched from their sisters. They had cried when they were robbed from their brothers. They had cried when they were in the guts of that disgusting ship, sardined between the dead and the dying, that horrible Middle Passage. They had cried. They were all cried out now. They wanted to go home.

They walked into that river and drowned themselves, every man, woman, and child, every infant without a whimper, without a word, without a cry. One itty bitty baby opened his mouth as if to wail. His momma softly and so tenderly suckled that babe. Everyone's head was held high. Not a face moved.

They walked into the water and stayed down.

That day the sea turned ebony.

They wanted to go home.

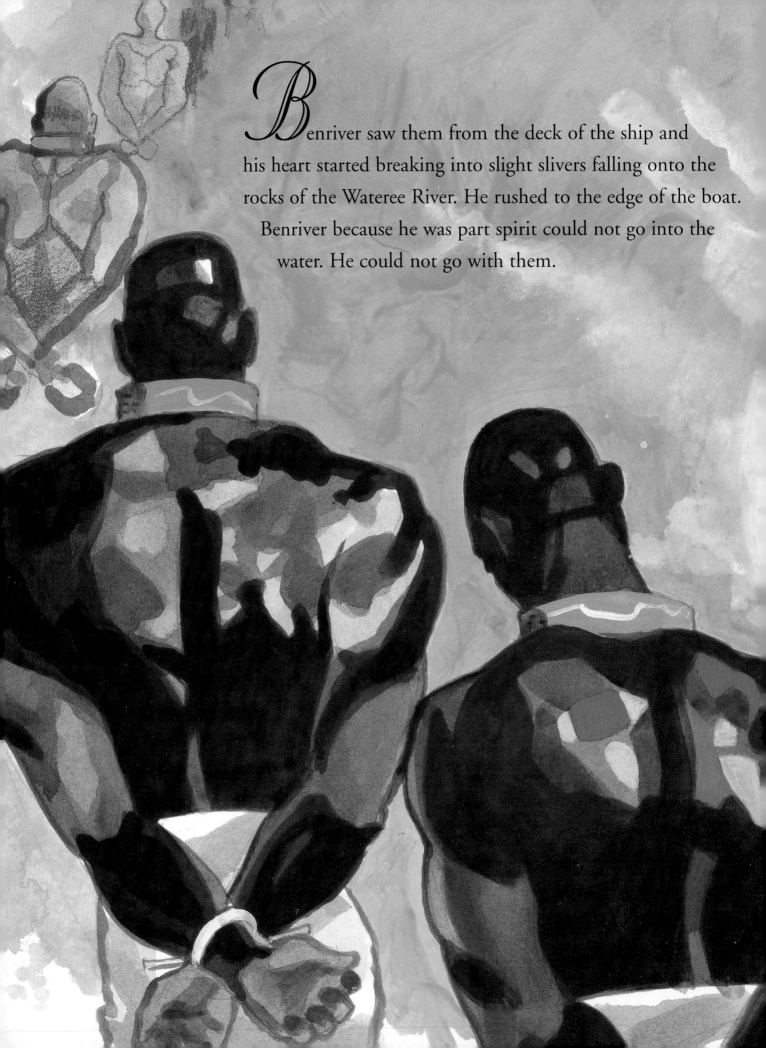

*B*enriver saw them from the deck of the ship and his heart started breaking into slight slivers falling onto the rocks of the Wateree River. He rushed to the edge of the boat. Benriver because he was part spirit could not go into the water. He could not go with them.

But he did not want to be left alone. He wanted to go home too.

lease, please," he pleaded. "Please, please," he begged. "Please, please," he shrieked in his African tongue. But they did not stop. And so he screeched, "Stop! Stop! Please, please, *pleeaasse,*" and his screams were heard around the world, but they would not stop. They wanted to go home.

It is said that the old stand between this world and the next. Auntie Louisa, an old slave standing near the boat, grabbed Benriver and held him tight. Auntie Louisa's face had lines where sorrow had plowed deep furrows. "You holds me chile and I'll holds you," she whispered hoarsely. "Slaves in this here land has just two choices: to live or to die. There's no shame in living. Every person must make his'n or her'n choice. Each person can choose onliest for hisself. You holds me chile and I'll holds you." And they held on to each other and cried for each other.

66 You are the keeper," Auntie Louisa told him. "You are the keeper of the dreams, the hopes, the stories, the hearts, the souls, the cries and the voices. You are the keeper."

The slave masters were at first silent too, dumbfounded. Not believing what they had just seen. Not believing what they didn't hear. There had not been one cry from the African Ebos fresh off the boat. There had not been one word from the seasoned slaves who had watched and understood. The slave masters were silent too. Then they started ranting and raving, screaming and crying about all the money they had just lost.

*I*f you go down to the banks of the Wateree River, you might still find Benriver there. He's an old man now. He has a long white cowtail, which is tied with a red ribbon on his head and hangs down his back. Over this he wears a three-cocked hat with peacock feathers, and a rose cockade with a bunch of ripe persimmons with three pods of red peppers as a top knot. Around his neck he wears a long, long sky-blue scarf that drapes to his knees, and he has a snake's skin in his pocket. Benriver is the best eyeservant on the plantation, always looking like he's working when he ain't doing nothing at all.

Benriver always says: "The day the sea turned ebony, they buried my heart on the banks of the Wateree. One day my heart is going to float back home to Africa on the waves of the Wateree River."

And the waves keep rolling, to and fro, to and fro.
Swoosh, swash, swish, swoosh,
swash, swish, splish, splash,
splish-splash
splatter.

Children walking along the banks of the Wateree
River call to him:

Hoodoo Man, Hoodoo Man,
Fix me a spell as fast as you can.

And he answers:

First you must remember
so you can never forget.
First you must remember.

And he tells them the story of Ebo Landing, of the
day the sea turned ebony, of those proud Africans
who simply wanted to go home.

$\mathcal{A}$nd the waves keep rolling,
to and fro, to and fro.
Swoosh, swash, swish,
swoosh,
swash,
swish,
splish, splash,
splish, splash,
splatter.